THIS BOOK BELONGS TO

_____

_____

WE ARE
ALL UNDER
ONE WIDE SKY

For every child, everywhere,
under one wide sky
—D.W.

For Marlene,
You can make the world a better place!
—A.S.

Sounds True
Boulder, CO 80306

Text © 2021 Deborah Wiles
Illustrations © 2021 Andrea Stegmaier

Published 2021

Book design by Ranée Kahler

Printed in South Korea

Library of Congress Cataloging-in-Publication Data

Names: Wiles, Deborah, author. | Stegmaier, Andrea, illustrator.
Title: We are all under one wide sky / by Deborah Wiles ; illustrated by
   Andrea Stegmaier.
Description: Boulder, CO : Sounds True, 2021. | Audience: Ages 4-8. |
   Summary: From two clouds to ten whirligigs to two sleepyheads, counts
   ordinary things that show how small our planet is and that, no matter
   where we live, we are connected under one wide sky.
Identifiers: LCCN 2020032409 (print) | LCCN 2020032410 (ebook) |
   ISBN 9781683646334 (hardback) | ISBN 9781683646341 (ebook)
Subjects: CYAC: Stories in rhyme. | Counting.
Classification: LCC PZ8.3.W6633 We 2021 (print) | LCC PZ8.3.W6633 (ebook)
   | DDC [E]--dc23
LC record available at https://lccn.loc.gov/2020032409
LC ebook record available at https://lccn.loc.gov/2020032410

10 9 8 7 6 5 4 3 2 1

WE ARE ALL UNDER ONE WIDE SKY

DEBORAH WILES   ANDREA STEGMAIER

sounds true
BOULDER, COLORADO

We are all under one wide sky.

Two clouds glide by.

Three songbirds sail the air.

Four fir trees over there.

Five feathers from a nest.

Six tulips bloom their best.

Seven dump trucks full of sand.

Eight bumblebees make a band.

Nine clovers for a crown.

Ten whirligigs spinning 'round.

Nine shadows butter the yard.

Eight fence posts standing guard.

Seven moonflowers open wide.

Six crickets creep inside.

Five lanterns softly glow.

Four gigglers in a row.

Three kisses, soft and sweet

Two sleepyheads fast asleep

Under . . .

one wide sky.

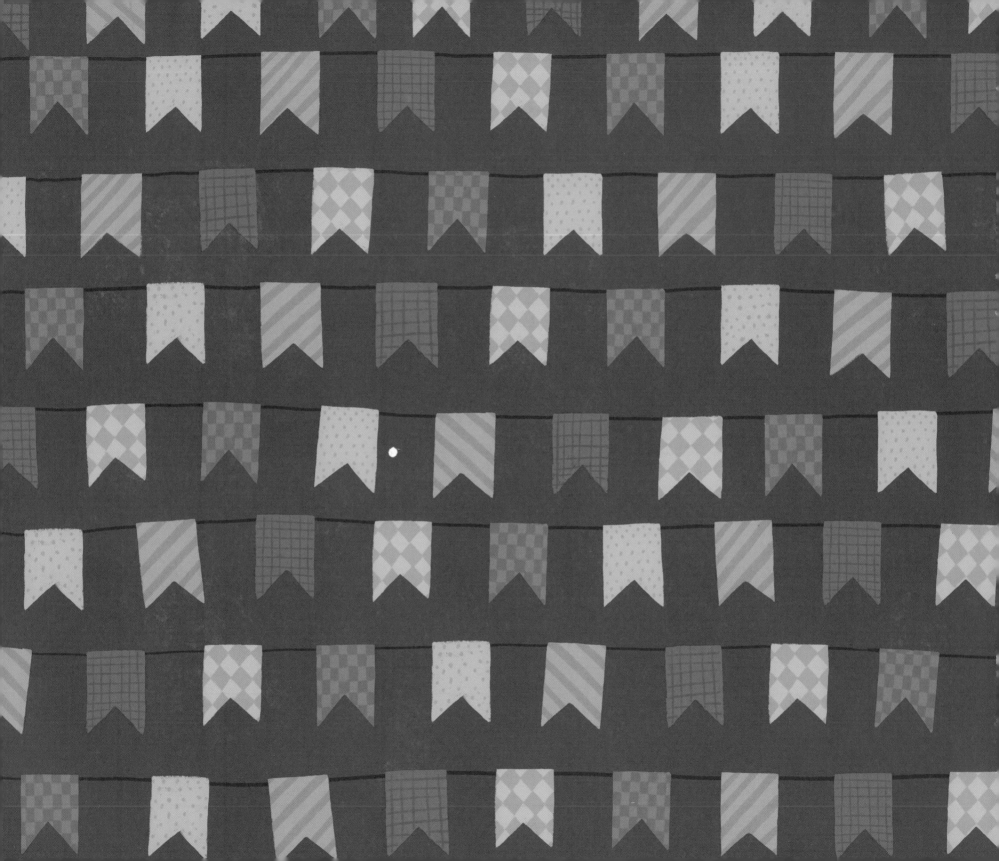